CHICAGO PUBLIC LIBRARY
SULZER REGIONAL
4455 N. LINCOLN
CHICAGO, IL 60625

JUV/
RC
606.65
.R445
2005

SULZER

APR 2006

DEADLY DISASTERS

The AIDS Epidemic

Disaster & Survival

Jennifer Reed

Enslow Publishers, Inc.
40 Industrial Road   PO Box 38
Box 398   Aldershot
Berkeley Heights, NJ 07922   Hants GU12 6BP
USA   UK
http://www.enslow.com

Copyright © 2005 by Enslow Publishers, Inc.

All rights reserved.

No part of this book may be reproduced by any means without the written permission of the publisher.

Library of Congress Cataloging-in-Publication Data

Reed, Jennifer.
   The AIDS epidemic : disaster & survival / Jennifer Bond Reed.
     p. cm. — (Deadly Disasters)
   Includes bibliographical references and index.
   ISBN 0-7660-2382-6
   1. AIDS (Disease)—Juvenile literature. I. Title. II. Series.
   RC606.65R445 2004
   616.97'92—dc22
                                          2004011699

Printed in the United States of America

10 9 8 7 6 5 4 3 2 1

To Our Readers: We have done our best to make sure all Internet addresses in this book were active and appropriate when we went to press. However, the author and the publisher have no control over and assume no liability for the material available on those Internet sites or on other Web sites they may link to. Any comments or suggestions can be sent by e-mail to comments@enslow.com or to the address on the back cover.

Illustration Credits: Associated Press, AP, pp. 1, 4, 7, 9, 10, 16, 19, 23, 28, 29, 32, 33, 35; Centers for Disease Control, p. 37; Enslow Publishers, Inc., p. 12; Kairos, Latin Stock/Science Photo Library, p. 14; National Archives and Records Administration, p. 24; Painet Photos, pp. 39, 40; Photos.com, p. 18; UN/DPI Photo, p. 25.

Cover Illustration: Associated Press, AP

Contents

1 AIDS: An African Nightmare 5

2 What is HIV/AIDS? 11

3 AIDS in Asia 21

4 AIDS in the U.S. 26

5 The Innocent 31

6 There Is Hope 36

The World's Deadliest Diseases
and Epidemics 41

Chapter Notes 42

Glossary 46

Further Reading and Internet Addresses .. 47

Index 48

AIDS activists rally in Cape Town, South Africa in 2003. They are protesting President Thabo Mbeki's lack of action to curb the spread of the disease.

CHAPTER 1

AIDS: An African Nightmare

IMAGINE BEING DEATHLY ILL, BUT NOT HAVING ANY medicine. The nearest hospital is hundreds of miles away and you are without a car. In North America, most people are able to receive treatment fairly quickly for their illnesses. However, this is not the case in Africa, Asia, and South America, where receiving medicine and treatment can be quite difficult.

A deadly disease is attacking people. Treating everyone is impossible. There is no cure. Every day, hundreds of people die while many more contract the disease.

AIDS is that disease. It does not matter what skin color people have, where they live or what religion they practice. AIDS kills men and women, boys and girls. It destroys lives, orphans children, and is spreading rapidly.

The AIDS Epidemic

What is AIDS?

AIDS stands for **A**cquired **I**mmune **D**eficiency **S**yndrome. "Acquired" means that a person can become infected with it. "Immune deficiency" means that the body is weakened to fight disease. "Syndrome" is a group of health problems that make up the disease.[1] A person is first infected with HIV usually through sexual activity, sharing drug needles, or acquiring the virus through a blood transfusion. HIV stands for **H**uman **I**mmunodeficiency **V**irus. A person with HIV will experience a weakening of the immune system, which helps fight disease. Illnesses that take advantage of the weakened immune system are called opportunistic illnesses. Once a person gets one of these illnesses and has significantly less CD4 cells (a special kind of white blood cell that attacks illnesses) than normal, he or she has developed AIDS.

AIDS is spreading quickly in Africa. It has orphaned more than 10 million children in Sub-Saharan Africa.[2] By 2010, there may be 30 million more orphans.

Esther's Day

Esther Daiton rises before dawn, rushes to the toilet outside her shack, and throws up. She has AIDS. Her father, mother, and two older sisters have already died from the disease. After the birth of her daughter, it was discovered through a blood test that Esther too had AIDS. Her daughter also had AIDS and died at the age of two. Esther not only has to take care of herself, but she takes care of other family members who have the disease.[3]

Because Esther lives in a remote village in Africa, she does not have access to a hospital or doctor. She cannot work because the pain is so bad. She cannot afford medicine. She worries about her family and wonders who will take care of them when she dies.

The AIDS epidemic in Zambia, Africa, has devastated the family structure. The southern half of the country now

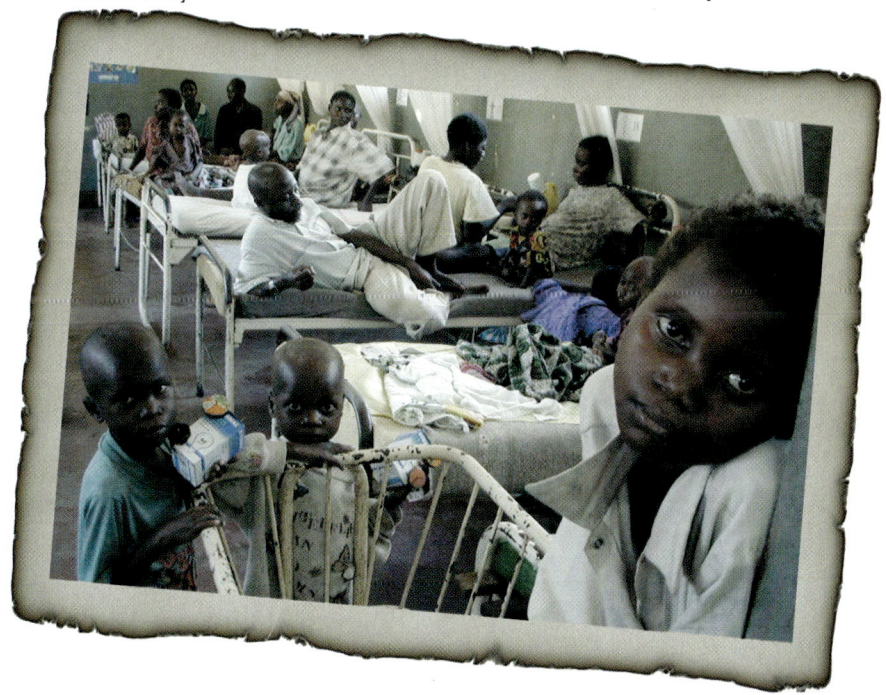

There are millions of orphans in Africa. Many of these orphans lost their parents to AIDS. They are awaiting treatment in a hospital in the Congo.

The AIDS Epidemic

has half a million orphans. Death from AIDS leaves children without a mother or a father. Suzanne Matale at the Christian Council of Churches in Zambia said, "Many of the orphans have no place to live and no one to care for them." About 20% of Zambia's population, or one in every five persons, is infected with AIDS.[4] The AIDS problem is worse in Zambia than other parts of the world. It is difficult to find jobs. The government does not help its people by sending them money. Without money, they cannot buy medicine or seek treatment.

Street Children of Angola

War has destroyed areas like Angola, Africa. Children were already suffering because of a civil war. Then, AIDS hit the area. Many street children of Angola are orphans. Because of the lack of money and jobs, families are turning away their own children. They survive by selling goods, begging, and stealing.

The street children with HIV suffer the most. Most will never make it to adulthood. Many will die in the streets that they called home all because of HIV and AIDS.

AIDS and the World

Throughout the world, AIDS has robbed more than 5 million children of one or both parents. Every minute, five young people contract HIV.[5] Every day, more than seventy-five

AIDS: An African Nightmare

These street children are looking for food in garbage bins in Luanda, Angola. In 1999, it was estimated that there were five thousand street children in Luanda alone. Many of them have lost their parents to AIDS or have AIDS themselves.

thousand people are infected. Today, HIV is transmitted in all countries.

Not everyone gives in to his or her disease. Catherine Phiri is HIV positive. An AIDS activist, she helps orphans in Malawi, Africa. Phiri set up a group that offers counseling, places orphans in good families, and takes blood to be tested for the virus. She has won an award from the United Nations for her work but still, "People look at me like trash," she said. "Sometimes when I go to sleep I fear

The AIDS Epidemic

Mark King is an AIDS educator from Atlanta, Georgia. He stands in front of a diagram of the AIDS virus. Educating people about how to prevent the transmission of HIV helps stop the spread of AIDS.

for the future of my children. But I will not run away now. Talking about it: that's what's brave."[6]

Controlling AIDS starts with knowledge. The United States has a much lower rate of infection because programs and education are in place. Africa, Asia, and South America are working to improve education. However, no matter what region, the struggle to find a cure and educate people continues to this day.

CHAPTER 2

What is HIV/AIDS?

BECAUSE AIDS HAS SPREAD ALL OVER THE WORLD, affecting millions of people, it is an epidemic. An epidemic is something that affects a large part of a population, community, or region. At the time of the AIDS outbreak, contagious diseases were at an all-time low. Contagious disease epidemics of the past include the influenza epidemic of 1918–1919. This was the most devastating epidemic in the twentieth century. Also known as Spanish Influenza, the outbreak killed more than five hundred thousand people.[1]

In parts of Asia and Africa, HIV/AIDS is also referred to as a pandemic. Pandemic means that something occurs over a wide geographic area and affects an exceptionally high portion of the population. Thailand and Zambia both have an AIDS pandemic.

The AIDS Epidemic

Epidemics

Today, many diseases have vaccinations and are no longer a problem in the United States. However, in other countries where medicine is not available, the diseases can become epidemics.

The chances of a new epidemic occurring are very real. In the spring of 2003, a disease known as SARS, severe acute respiratory syndrome, struck in China. It quickly spread to other parts of Asia as well as Toronto, Canada. By April 1, 2003, nearly two thousand people were reported to have SARS, and sixty-two people had

AIDS has become a global epidemic. Though Southern Africa and South Asia have the highest number of cases, the disease continues to be of grave concern throughout the world.

What is HIV/AIDS?

died.[2] By the end of April in countries like Canada and the United States, the rate of infections slowed. The disease spread to two dozen countries by air travel. Tourists and travelers from China brought home an infectious disease! The total amount of people infected according to the Centers for Disease Control and Prevention was 8,098 and total deaths reached 774.[3]

Unlike SARS, HIV and AIDS are not spread through the air. They are spread through the blood or sexual activity. But how did AIDS come into existence?

Monkeys and HIV

Before it became an epidemic, AIDS was an unknown disease that originated in Africa. The earliest sample of HIV-infected blood dates back to 1959 by an adult male living in what is now the Democratic Republic of Congo, Africa.[4] Scientists will probably never know exactly when and where the virus first appeared. By measuring the rate at which the virus has mutated since the epidemic first started, scientists at the Los Alamos National Laboratory calculate that HIV first appeared around 1930. Many scientists believe that the virus was transmitted from monkeys or chimpanzees to man. In parts of western Africa, where these animals are hunted for food, it is believed that the chimp's blood mixed with human blood during

The AIDS Epidemic

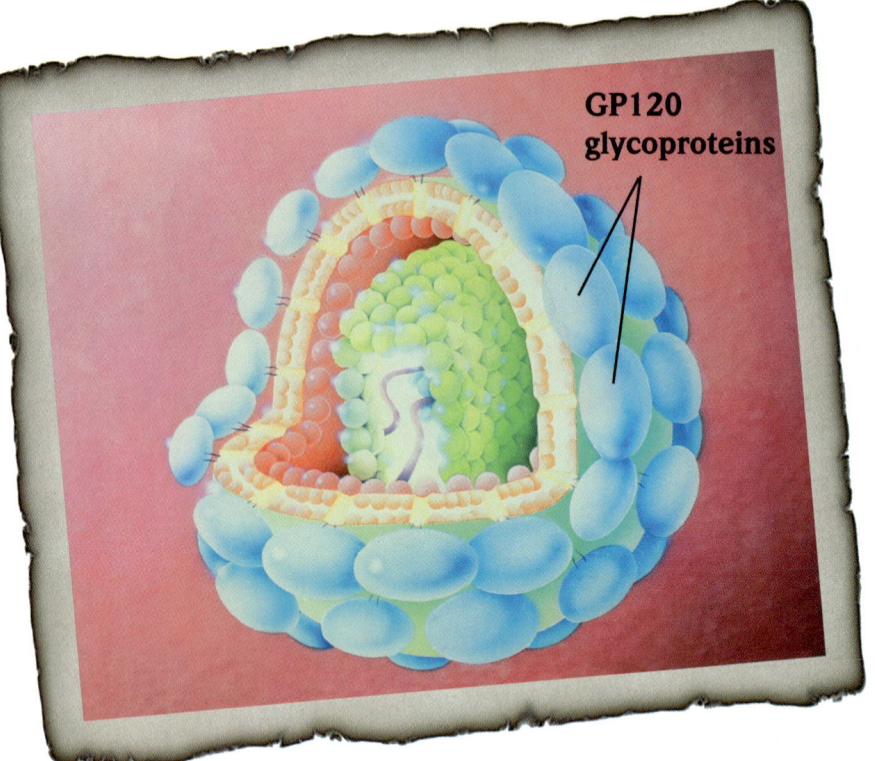

The HIV virus, which causes AIDS, attacks white blood cells. These cells normally protect the body from disease and infections. The GP120 glycoproteins on the outside of the HIV virus bind to the white blood cells.

hunting. Certain viruses can pass from animals to humans. This process is called zoonosis.[5]

HIV and AIDS

Blood tests are used to determine if a person has HIV. However if a person is HIV positive, it does not mean that he or she has AIDS.

What is HIV/AIDS?

The Centers for Disease Control and Prevention has set up some criteria to determine if a person has AIDS or not. People may be relatively healthy even though they have HIV. The virus changes and attacks the immune system in a person's body. If that person becomes sick, the body's ability to fight the illness is weakened. It cannot protect itself from an illness as common as a cold. HIV specifically attacks the cells that produce antibodies in a human body. A body produces billions of antibodies to combat viruses. AIDS occurs when a person shows signs that his or her immune system cannot fight back and is damaged. These signs include the presence of opportunistic illnesses, and a reduction in CD4 cells.

Symptoms

For many people it is sometimes months to years before they have any symptoms of AIDS. However, in infants, the symptoms occur much sooner, often within the first two years of their life. Because a baby's immune system is not fully developed at birth, it is much harder for a baby's body to fight disease. With HIV present, it is often impossible. If a mother has HIV, babies are tested to see if the virus is in their bodies. A blood test will tell the doctor if a baby has HIV.

The symptoms from HIV come from other infections like a cold, influenza or bacterial infection. Other viruses

The AIDS Epidemic

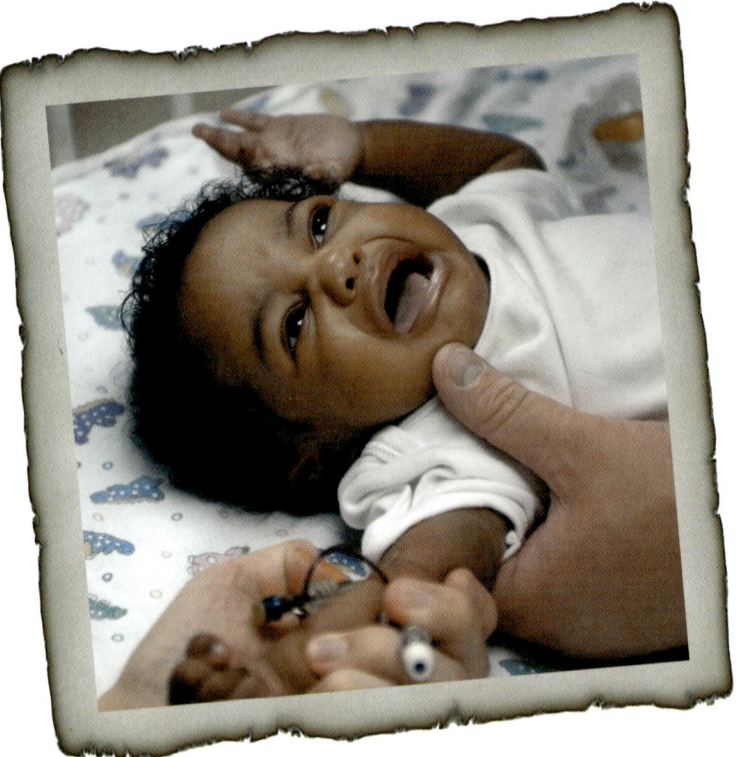

Babies of HIV- or AIDS-infected mothers have their blood tested to find out whether or not they have the disease.

and bacterial diseases such as herpes, tuberculosis, and hepatitis can harm the human body. When HIV is present, the body's ability to fight off the infection from these diseases is difficult. Adults may have flu-like symptoms in the beginning. These include fatigue, weight loss, skin rashes, and diarrhea. In children, some symptoms may be coughing, diarrhea, fever, night sweats, and headaches. These become worse as time goes on. Despite the presence

What is HIV/AIDS?

of these symptoms, however, only a blood test can confirm if a person is HIV positive.

A person with HIV can look and even feel normal. But when he or she becomes ill, it can be a fight for life. AIDS becomes deadly when the body has been so badly damaged by the virus that it cannot fight back when another illness strikes. For example, a cold could eventually lead to pneumonia. This could cause difficulty in breathing, which could lead to death.

How HIV is transmitted

When HIV was first discovered, many myths existed about how a person could get it. This caused fear among people. Some of these myths said that people could get HIV from kissing another infected person or sitting on an infected toilet. A person cannot get HIV by breathing the same air as an infected person, drinking the same water, or being bitten by a mosquito. It is also very rare for HIV/AIDS to be transmitted through the sweat and tears of an infected person.

HIV may be given to another person through fluids such as blood, semen, and mother's milk. It can also be transmitted from person to person through their blood by sharing needles. Many drug users are infected by the virus because they share infected needles.

Although now rare, HIV may be passed through blood

The AIDS Epidemic

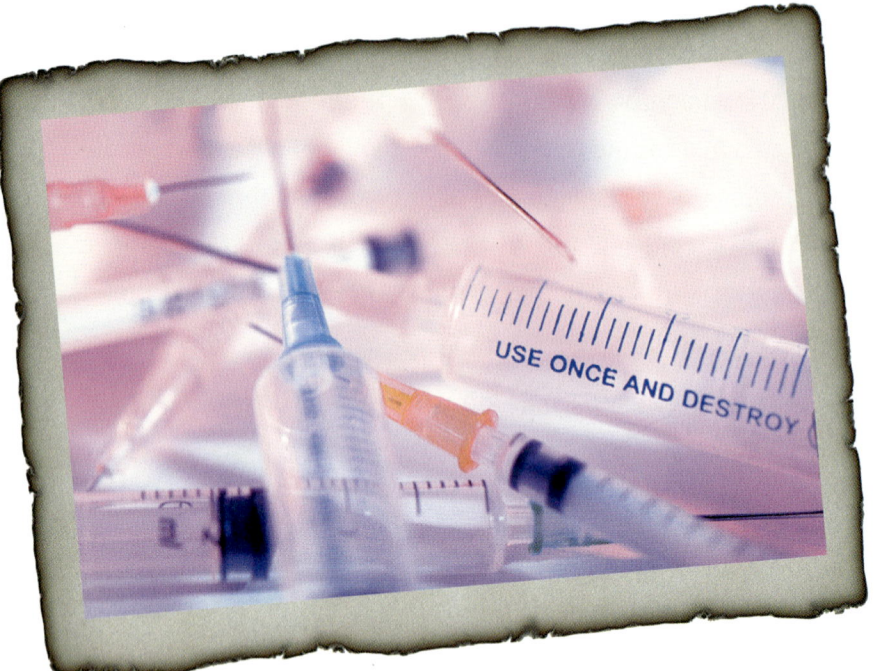

Many needles now have the instructions "Use once and destroy" written on their sides. Doctors and nurses know to throw out a needle after giving a shot or drawing blood. This helps prevent the spread of AIDS.

transfusions. Today, blood is tested to ensure that it is safe. It is also safe to give blood. All needles are either new or cleaned and sterilized before use.

Health-care workers also need to take precautions during surgeries. They wear latex gloves, masks, safety glasses, and full uniforms to help prevent infection.

Infected mothers may pass HIV to their babies during delivery or through breast-feeding. If a mother is HIV positive, she should not breast feed her baby.

What is HIV/AIDS?

Unprotected sexual intercourse or oral sex is another way the virus is passed. Without the use of a condom, an infected person is more likely to pass HIV to another person. A condom helps prevent the disease from being transmitted, but it is not 100 percent effective. Abstinence, or not having sexual intercourse or oral sex, is the safest form of prevention.

This three-month-old baby has HIV. His name is Joseph and he was abandoned by his parents. Now, he is cared for at the Nyumbani House in Karen, Kenya.

The AIDS Epidemic

Treatment

There are many ways to treat HIV and AIDS. The symptoms and problems vary depending on each person. Antiviral drugs like Retrovir, AZT, or Combivir have been proven effective in controlling symptoms. But they do not stop the disease. They help the body to recover normally from illness. These drugs stop HIV from changing the healthy material of cells. They keep the virus from spreading to new cells and decrease the virus in the body.[6]

Antibiotics may also be used as treatment for patients. They help fight bacterial infections. Eating healthy, vitamin-rich foods and exercising may also help patients live a longer and better life.

At this time, there is no cure for HIV/AIDS. Money and education are the keys to preventing the spread of HIV. In his 2003 State of the Union Address, President George W. Bush asked Congress to commit 15 billion dollars to "turn the tide against AIDS in the most afflicted nations of Africa and the Caribbean."

If this kind of dedication is acted upon, Americans and people all over the world can make a difference in the fight against HIV and AIDS.

CHAPTER 3

AIDS in Asia

ASIA IS ON THE BRINK OF A FULL-BLOWN AIDS epidemic. In the last ten years, HIV has established itself in all parts of Asia. It is spreading at a fast rate. By December 2003, UNAIDS estimated that 7.4 million people in Asia were living with HIV or AIDS.[1] Many of these people do not even know they are infected. India and Thailand have the largest amount of infected people.

In Asia, few people have heard of HIV and AIDS. Most do not understand what they are and how they spread. This is mainly due to a lack of education. Some people have HIV but do not know it. They may not have any symptoms. The symptoms that some have are similar to a more common disease such as the flu. As in Africa, HIV and AIDS are deeply misunderstood in Asia. By 2010, it is

The AIDS Epidemic

believed that at least 30 million people in China and India alone will be infected.[2]

Governments of some countries refuse to establish programs that would educate and help citizens with HIV. They avoid policies that confront sensitive social, cultural and moral issues.[3] Care and treatment for HIV and AIDS is low. Hospitals are not equipped to help the millions of people infected by the disease. Services and programs are not in place to offer help, education, and medicine.

Poverty and AIDS

HIV and AIDS affect people in poorer areas of the world more. In parts of Thailand, Cambodia, and Indonesia, many people suffer from malnutrition, illiteracy, and improper medical treatment. Fathers or mothers die, sometimes from AIDS, leaving a family with nothing. Because there is little money, it is difficult to buy food and many children go hungry. Without money, families cannot see a doctor and get medicine. When people are not fed properly, their immune system does not work as well. Add HIV and AIDS to a sick, malnourished body, along with lack of treatment, and death often comes quickly.

Children in Asia

Iwan lives on the street in Jakarta, Indonesia. He shines shoes, steals, and prostitutes himself. He also has HIV

AIDS in Asia

People in poorer areas of the world are more affected by AIDS. This family in Cambodia has no home.

because he never wore a condom after becoming sexually active. He has never heard about AIDS.[4]

Dede is fifteen years old. He dropped out of junior high and lives on the streets. He sleeps in bus terminals and has sex with prostitutes. Dede has heard about AIDS. He knows there is no cure. However, he never wears condoms.[5]

Nearly twenty thousand children live on the streets of Jakarta. The stories of these two children are similar to millions of others around Asia. Many children left home

The AIDS Epidemic

because they got into trouble. Some were sent away by parents who could not take care of them. Others were orphaned and had no place else to go.

They struggle day to day to survive. Often, these children turn to drugs and sexual exploitation for comfort and money. It is in this world that they often become infected with HIV.

Many street children do not realize they are killing

This heroin came from southwest Asia. The continent produces most of the world's heroin. This is because the poppy plant, where heroin comes from, is most easily grown there.

AIDS in Asia

themselves. They may share drug needles as well as have sex with infected people.

The AIDS epidemic in Southern Asia has spread fast among injecting drug users, including children. It is not difficult to find drugs in this area. Most of the world's opium and heroin are produced in Asia.

Despite the AIDS epidemic in Asia, there is help. Social services such as UNAIDS and Rescue/AIDS in Indonesia teach people about HIV and AIDS. Although many more will be infected and die, thousands will be saved through education.

UNAIDS has offices not just in Asia, but around the whole world. Here, a UNAIDS worker meets with a local woman who helps provide AIDS information to the public.

CHAPTER 4

AIDS in the U.S.

In 1981, when Josh was just a baby, he was diagnosed with hemophilia, a hereditary blood defect. The blood of people with this disease has difficulty clotting. Clotting helps to stop blood flow from a cut or wound. If blood cannot clot, or has a hard time clotting, a person might die from bleeding too much. This is called hemorrhaging.

Josh

Josh needed a blood transfusion. At the time of his transfusion, in the early eighties, little was known about AIDS. Those who donated blood in America were not tested for HIV.[1] When Josh received his blood transfusion, he also received HIV. His parents told Josh when he was six years old that he was HIV positive. At first, Josh led a normal life. He did not experience any problems with HIV. At age nine, he became very ill. Instead of attending summer camp like most kids, Josh was accepted into a research program at the National Institutes of Health. He was put on medication such as AZT, ddI, and 3TC. The medicines helped, but Josh could not gain weight. He stopped growing.[2]

Josh now has two deadly diseases—HIV and hemophilia. He says his life was lonely in the early years. No one knew his HIV status except family and teachers at school. When he was twelve, a rumor went around about Josh's HIV status. Rather than denying it, Josh made his illness public, but it cost him his best friend. His friend's father would not let his son see Josh anymore.[3]

Josh educated children and teens about his illness. He appeared on the Phil Donahue Show and became a public speaker. People accepted him more. They stopped treating him like a monster and more like a friend. He went to birthday parties and movies and hung out with friends.[4]

At age eighteen, Josh planned to go to college. He struggled with his illness. He relied on support groups and medication to keep him healthy.

People with HIV are still stigmatized today. Josh proved that even a little education on the subject can go a long way. He had the benefit of a supportive family, caring friends and support groups, hospitals and medications, proper nutrition, and a deep desire to live.

The AIDS Epidemic

Support groups help HIV-infected people cope with having the disease. They can talk to each other and can express their feelings about HIV and AIDS.

AIDS Deaths Drop in the U.S.

AIDS and HIV cases in North America and parts of Western Europe are fewer than in other parts of the world. In 1997, the Centers for Disease Control and Prevention (CDC) said that deaths in the United States dropped 13 percent in the first half of 1996 to about 22,000, down from 24,900 for the same period in 1995. The growth rate for people diagnosed with AIDS also slowed down. The CDC attributes the decreases to prevention education and

AIDS in the U.S.

new treatments. Although this is good news, many doctors remain cautious.[5]

New Therapies

In the United States, it seems that therapy, rather than behavioral change, was the main reason for the decline in new cases of HIV as well as the decline in deaths. HAART, highly active anti-retroviral therapy, is a therapy often used to treat HIV patients in the United States.[6] In 1999 and 2000, the total number of deaths from AIDS in the

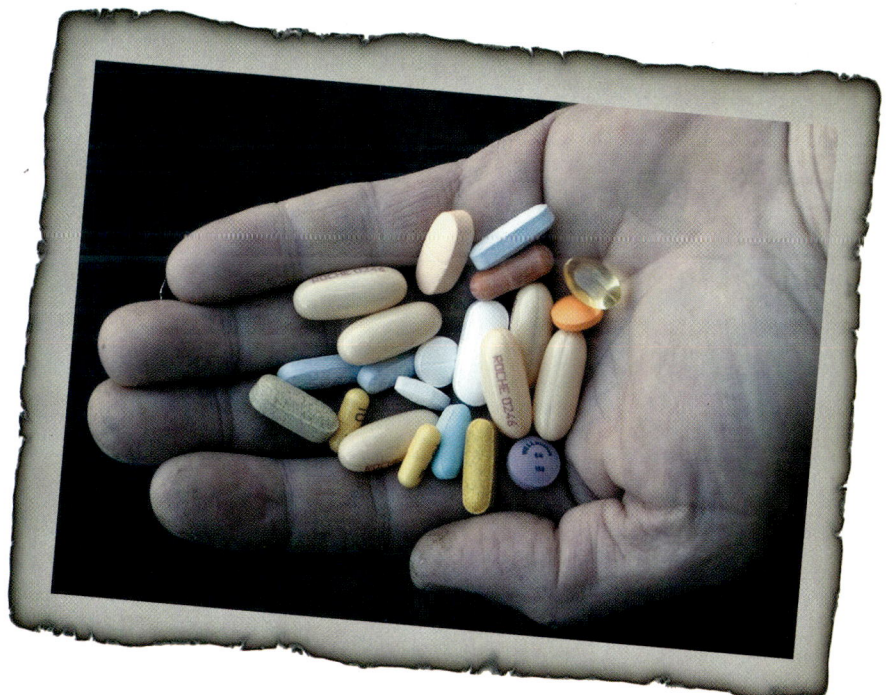

This is a mid-day dose of pills for an HIV-positive person. Many patients take almost fifty pills a day.

The AIDS Epidemic

United States was 467,910. The age group hardest hit was the 35–44 year age range.[7] The total number of people living with AIDS as of the year 2001 was 495,592.[8]

Losing Sight of the Danger

A documentary aired on VH-1 named *AIDS: A Pop Culture History*. The show stated that in recent years, AIDS cases have been on the rise. This popular music-television network asked some interesting questions regarding America's view of AIDS. To most, it is a problem in Africa but not in America. It has almost become a thing of the past. When television, movies, and music videos depict sex, when promiscuous behavior is seen as acceptable, chances are the cases of AIDS and other infectious diseases will begin to rise.[9] This is exactly what is happening in America today.

The Washington Post reported that, for the first time in 10 years, the number of AIDS cases has increased. There was a 2.2-percent rise in 2002.[10]

However, AIDS education in North America and parts of Western Europe continues to make a huge difference. Sometimes, the best educators are those people who have experienced the disease themselves.

Chapter 5

The Innocent

IN THE MID-1980S PEOPLE KNEW LITTLE ABOUT AIDS and HIV. What they did know stemmed from fear, lies, and rumors. Many thought it was the gay man's disease and only homosexual men contracted it. Gay singer Freddy Mercury of the band Queen died from the disease. Gay Olympic diver Greg Louganis revealed that he has AIDS in 1995. The disease was called GRID—Gay Related Immuno Deficiency. AIDS became more than just a contagious disease. So when a teen boy contracted HIV, he aimed to let the world know that anyone could get the disease.

AIDS at Thirteen

Ryan White was born in 1971, and just days after his birth, doctors told his parents that he was a hemophiliac.

The AIDS Epidemic

Greg Louganis (center) won the gold medal for diving in the 1988 Summer Olympics. Here he is receiving his medal.

When he was thirteen years old, he had pneumonia. Ryan had to have an operation removing two inches of his left lung. He also had to have a blood transfusion. This blood infected him with HIV. Ryan's parents were told after the operation that he now had AIDS. His hemophilia plus HIV equaled AIDS. With two deadly diseases, doctors gave Ryan only six months to live.

"I came face to face with death at thirteen years old," Ryan said. "I was diagnosed with AIDS: a killer. . . . Given six months to live and being the fighter that I am, I set

The Innocent

high goals for myself. It was my decision to live a normal life, go to school, be with my friends, and enjoy day to day activities. It was not going to be easy."[1] Ryan fought his disease and the discrimination that followed. The town where he lived did not support him. Residents at school board meetings announced that their children would not

This photo of Ryan White was taken in 1988, two years before he died.

The AIDS Epidemic

be allowed in the same classroom as Ryan.[2] He was forced to use a separate bathroom. The cafeteria gave him disposable silverware and other students vandalized his locker. He could not participate in gym class. He had to drink from a separate water fountain. Then, his school banned him from attending. People were afraid because they did not understand the disease. Hate, fear, and discrimination plagued his town.

A New Life

Ryan and his mother moved to Cicero, Indiana. There, people had been educated about AIDS and accepted Ryan. In fact, many people embraced Ryan and his story. He appeared on talk shows and the news. A movie was made about his fight, not just against AIDS, but also against discrimination. It was called *The Ryan White Story*. He became the poster child for AIDS victims. Ryan made it his goal to educate as many people as possible about AIDS. He showed the world that you do not have to be a homosexual to have the disease. Even a young boy could contract HIV through a legitimate medical procedure. Ryan became a national hero. AIDS was no longer a moral issue but a disease that could be contracted by anyone.

> "I came face to face with death at thirteen years old. . . ."
>
> —Ryan White, AIDS sufferer and activist.

The Innocent

Safe-sex kits provide important information on the prevention of AIDS. Kits like the one at the right were distributed to members of the Navajo Nation.

Ryan White died on April 8, 1990 at the age of eighteen. He had accomplished more than most teens his age. Today, many people are better educated about HIV and AIDS thanks in part to Ryan White and his story.

AIDS and the Media

Partially because of the awareness raised in the 1980s by Ryan White, AIDS reached the mainstream media by the 1990s. The movie *Philadelphia*, starring Tom Hanks, featured an HIV-positive main character. Musicians promoted safe sex and monogamous (dating one person at a time) relationships. People were more willing to openly talk about safe sex and the use of condoms or abstinence without feeling embarrassed.[3] As their disease began to be discussed in the open, many AIDS sufferers looked to new treatments for hope.

Chapter 6

There Is Hope

According to the Joint United Nations Programme on HIV/AIDS, at the end of 2003, almost 40 million people were estimated to have HIV/AIDS. Thirty-seven million are adults. Two-and-a-half million are children under fifteen. An estimated five million people acquired HIV in 2002.[1]

In the Laboratories

However, there is hope. Many nations such as the United States and countries in Africa are dedicated to helping people and finding a cure. Clinical trials (tests) are taking place on a vaccine that seems to have at least a partial effect on the virus. Thousands of people infected with the virus volunteer to have these tests done. Without their

There Is Hope

help, a vaccine may never be found. Dr. Anthony Fauci at the National Health Institute said that even a modest effect could have a good impact in countries with high rates of AIDS.[2] Most experts believe that a vaccine is the only way to stop the virus from spreading. Finding it may be ten or more years away.

In western countries, medicines such as antiviral drugs are easily accessible. They help AIDS patients. But in developing countries in Africa and Asia, the drugs are too expensive and hard to find. Until a vaccine is discovered, scientists are looking for a way to provide affordable treatment for everyone.

Dr. Robert Gallo, director of the Institute of Human Virology at the University of Maryland and co-discoverer of HIV, is taking a different approach. Rather than trying to understand how the virus operates, Dr. Gallo and his team focus on the immune

Scientist Carol Reed conducts AIDS research for the Centers for Disease Control and Prevention.

37

The AIDS Epidemic

system itself. They are trying to understand how the immune system responds to the virus. Their focus is on naturally occurring chemicals in the body called chemokines. Chemokines are tiny molecules involved in communication among immune system cells. Gallo and his team have found that some chemokines are able to block HIV infection.[3]

Other scientists are looking elsewhere to help HIV and AIDS victims. Rather than finding a vaccine to stop the virus, they want to control it. A good example of how this works is with the polio vaccine, which all children in the United States receive. The polio virus enters the body and makes its way to the spinal cord where it causes the disease. The polio vaccine does not prevent the polio virus from entering the blood. It just slows it down enough to keep it from entering the spinal cord and causing neurological disease. Scientists are looking for ways to control HIV once it has entered the body.

> "It was my decision to live a normal life. . ."
>
> —Ryan White, AIDS sufferer and activist.

Red Ribbon Campaign

Many programs help HIV/AIDS victims. Fundraisers, AIDS Awareness Days, the HIV/AIDS quilt, and special programs are some examples of how people show their support to families and friends who are infected. People

There Is Hope

Each section of the AIDS Memorial Quilt is devoted to one person who died from the disease.

also show their support by wearing a red ribbon. The Red Ribbon was created in 1991 by the Visual AIDS Artists Caucus in New York. This ribbon stands for care and concern, hope and support.

World AIDS Day

World AIDS Day is December 1 of each year.[4] It was created by the World Summit of Ministers of Health on Programmes for AIDS Prevention in January 1998. It has strengthened the exchange of information and experience

The AIDS Epidemic

People are encouraged to wear Red Ribbons on World AIDS Day and any other day to show their support for those suffering with AIDS.

and encouraged tolerance. Since its creation, World AIDS Day has received the support of the World Health Assembly; the United Nations; and governments, communities, and individuals around the world.

Each year there is a new theme for this special day. In 2003, the theme was *Live and Let Live*. The day brings messages of hope, compassion and understanding about AIDS to every country in the world.

The World's Deadliest Diseases and Epidemics

Disease	Description
Cholera	A bacterial disease. It is an epidemic in Latin America and Africa today.
Ebola	A viral disease. Found today only in parts of Africa, it is a deadly disease with no cure. It was brought to Reston, Virginia, via monkeys, but did not spread to humans.
Hepatitis	A viral disease. As many as three hundred thousand people in the U.S. have hepatitis.
Influenza	A viral disease. There is a vaccine but new strains of influenza are on the rise. The biggest outbreak of influenza was the Spanish Flu of 1918–1919, which killed 20 million people.
Plague	Caused by bacteria and transmitted through rats and rodents. The Black Death plague started in Asia and was carried west by ships to Europe. By the end, around 1400, it is believed that about half of Europe's population had died.
Smallpox	A viral disease which was eliminated in America. Although there is a vaccine, it has not been regularly administered in years. The threat of bioterrorism in the twenty-first century has made people more aware of this deadly disease.
Tuberculosis	A bacterial disease. Affected a large number of the population in the United States in the mid-nineteenth century due to overcrowded cities and poor sanitary conditions. Though there is a vaccine today, it is still a problem in many parts of the world.

Chapter Notes

Chapter 1. AIDS: An African Nightmare

1. AIDS.Org, "AIDS Fact Sheet: What is AIDS?," *AIDS.Org*, n.d., <http://www.aids.org/FactSheets/101-what-is-aids.html> (November 14, 2003).

2. Simon Robinson, "Orphan of AIDS," *Time Magazine*, December 13, 1999, <http://www.time.com/time/archive/preview/from_search/0,10987,1101991213-35505,00.html> (November 21, 2003).

3. Ibid.

4. General Board of Global Ministries, "AIDS in Africa: Heartbreak and Hope," *United Methodist Committee on Relief*, n.d., <http://gbgm-umc.org/health/aidsafrica/> (November 21, 2003).

5. Alice Park, "AIDS Update: Suffer the Children," *Time Magazine*, July 10, 2000, <http://www.time.com/time/archive/preview/from_search/0,10987,1101000710-49058,00.html> (November 21, 2003).

6. Simon Robinson, "A Fighter in a Land of Orphans," *Time Magazine*, 2001, <http://www.time.com/time/2001/aidsinafrica/fighter.html> (November 21, 2003).

Chapter 2. What is HIV/AIDS?

1. Encyclopedia Britannica: Epidemics, n.d., <http://search.britannica.com/search?ref=B04319&query=epidemic> (November 22, 2003).

2. "Summary of Severe Acute Respiratory Syndrome Cases, Canada and International: April 2003," April 2003, <http://www.hc-sc.gc/pphb-dgspsp/sarssras/euae/sars20030402_e.html#international> (November 21, 2003).

3. Centers for Disease Control and Prevention, "Basic

Chapter Notes

Information About SARS," n.d., <http://www.cdc.gov/ncidod/sars/factsheet.htm> (November 21, 2003).

4. Alice Park, "When Did AIDS Begin?," *Time Magazine*, February 14, 2000, <http://www.time.com/time/archive/preview/from_search/0,10987,1101000214-38824,00.html> (April 12, 2004).

5. Annabel Kanabus and Sarah Allen, "The Origins of AIDS and HIV," *Avert.org*, n.d., <http://www.avert.org/origins.htm> (November 22, 2003).

6. Centers for Disease Control and Prevention, "What is AIDS?," n.d., <http://www.cdc.gov/hiv/pubs/faq/faq2.htm> (November 24, 2003).

Chapter 3. AIDS in Asia

1. UNAIDS, "Asia and the Pacific," *AIDS Epidemic Update: December 2003*, November 25, 2003, <http://www.unaids.org/wad/2003/Epiudate2003_en/Epi03_06_en.htm> (March 23, 2004).

2. UNAIDS, "Asian Harm Reduction Network," *UNAIDS.org*, n.d., <http://www.unaids.org/wac/2002/AsianHarmReductionNetwork.html> (March 23, 2004).

3. Edward Haugh and Indu Bhushan, "AIDS: Asia's Lull Before the Storm?," *Asian Development Bank*, n.d., <http://www.adb.org/Documents/Periodicals/ADB_Review/2001/vol33_3/AIDS.asp> (April 12, 2004).

4. Bill Black and Arin P. Farrington, "Preventing HIV/AIDS by Promoting Life for Indonesian Street Children," *AIDScaptions, Volume IV, No 1*, July 1997, <http://www.fhi.org/en/hivaids/Publications/Archive/Articles/AIDScaptions/volume4no1/IndonesiaStChildren.htm> (April 12, 2004).

The AIDS Epidemic

5. Ibid.

Chapter 4. AIDS in the U.S.

1. Body Positive, "Josh: Living with HIV Since He Was Four Years Old," *The Body: An AIDS and HIV Information Resource, Volume XII, Number 8*, August 1999, <http://www.thebody.com/bp/aug99/josh.html> (December 7, 2003).

2. Ibid.

3. Ibid.

4. Ibid.

5. Centers for Disease Control and Prevention, "Table 20. Deaths in persons with AIDS, by race/ethnicity, age at death, and sex, occurring in 1999 and 2000; and cumulative totals reported through December 2001, United States," *HIV/AIDS Surveillance Report, Volume 13, Number 2*, n.d, <http://www.cdc.gov/hiv/stats/hasr1302/table20.htm> (December 7, 2003).

6. J.M. Karon, P.L. Flemin, R.W. Steketee, and K.M. De Cock, "HIV in the United States at the Turn of the Century: An Epidemic in Transition," *American Journal of Public Health*, Volume 91 (7), June 2001, pp. 1060–1068.

7. Centers for Disease Control and Prevention, "Table 1. Persons reported to be living with HIV infection and with AIDS, by state and age group, reported through December 2001," *HIV/AIDS Surveillance Report, Volume 13, Number 2*, n.d., <http://www.cdc.gov/hiv/stats/hasr1302/table1.htm> (December 7, 2003).

8. Ibid.

9. VH-1 News, "AIDS: A Pop Culture History," *VH-1.com*, n.d., <http://www.vh1.com/shows/dyn/vh1_news_

Chapter Notes

presents/74420/episode_about.jhtml> (December 7, 2003).

10. Rob Stein, "AIDS cases in U.S. Increase," *Washington Post*, July 29, 2003, p. A01.

Chapter 5. The Innocent

1. Ryan White's Testimony before the President's Commission on AIDS, n.d., <sources.wikipedia.org/wiki.cgi?Ryan_White%27s_Testimony_Before_The_President%27s_Commission_On_AIDS> (December 7, 2003).

2. VH-1 News, "AIDS: A Pop Culture History," *VH-1.com*, n.d., <http://www.vh1.com/shows/dyn/vh1_news_presents/74420/episode_about.jhtml> (December 7, 2003).

3. Ibid.

Chapter 6. There Is Hope

1. Centers for Disease Control and Prevention, "Basic Statistics," <www.cdc.gov/hiv/stats.htm> (December 7, 2003).

2. "AIDS Vaccine May be 10 Years Away," *The New York Times*, March 15, 2002, <www.nytimes.com> (December 7, 2003).

3. Elizabeth Arledge, "The Virus Fighter," *Nova Online*, n.d., <http://www.pbs.org/wgbh/nova/aids/fighters.html> (December 7, 2003).

4. UNAIDS <http://www.unaids.org> (December 7, 2003).

Glossary

AIDS—Acquired Immune Deficiency Syndrome; a severe manifestation of infection with the human immunodeficiency virus (HIV).

antibodies—Cells that the body naturally produces to fight off disease and infection.

antiviral—Able to fight against viral infections.

CD4 cell—A special type of white blood cell that attacks illnesses.

chemokines—Tiny molecules involved in communication among cells engaged in immune response.

contagious—Communicable by contact. Easily spread through contact.

epidemic—Something that affects or tends to affect a large number of individuals within a population, community, or region at the same time.

hemophilia—A blood defect where the blood has difficulty clotting. Can lead to death.

hemorrhaging—When blood cannot clot.

HIV—Human Immunodeficiency Virus; an infectious disease which breaks down the immune system; the cause of AIDS.

opportunistic illness—An illness that takes advantage of a person's weakened immune system.

pandemic—Occurring over a wide geographic area and affecting a high percentage of the population.

Sub-Saharan Africa—The part of Africa that is south of the Saharan Desert.

vaccine—A substance that stimulates a response from the immune system to fight against disease.

zoonosis—The process that allows certain viruses to be passed from animals to humans.

Further Reading

Books

Check, William A.; introduction by C. Everett Koop. *AIDS*. Philadelphia: Chelsea House Pub., 1999.

Guest, Emma. *Children of AIDS: Africa's Orphan Crisis.* London: Pluto Press, 2003.

Houle, Michelle M. *AIDS in the 21st Century: What You Should Know.* Berkeley Heights, N.J.: Enslow Publishers, Inc., 2003.

Packer, Kenneth L. *HIV Infection: The Facts You Need to Know.* New York: Franklin F. Watts, 1998.

Schulman, Arlene. *Carmine's Story: A Book About a Boy Living with AIDS.* Minneapolis: Lerner Publications, 1997.

Whelan, Jo. *AIDS*. Austin, Tex.: Raintree Steck-Vaughn, 2002.

Internet Addresses

The AIDS Memorial Quilt
<http://www.aidsquilt.org/>

Centers for Disease Control and Prevention—Divisions of HIV/AIDS Prevention
<http://www.cdc.gov/hiv/dhap.htm>

UNAIDS: The Joint United Nations Program on HIV/AIDS
<http://www.unaids.org/en/default.asp>

Index

A
AIDS (Acquired Immune Deficiency Syndrome), 6
and the media, 35
death statistics, 28–29
diagnosis of, 14–15
discrimination, 10, 27, 33–34
education, 10, 20, 21, 25, 27, 30, 34, 35
in Africa, 5–10, 11, 20, 36, 37
in Asia, 5, 11, 21–25, 37
infection statistics, 8, 9, 21, 22, 29–30, 36
in the United States, 10, 26–30, 36
support for victims of, 38–39
symptoms of, 15
treatment of, 20, 29
antibiotics, 20
antibodies, 15
antiviral drugs, 20, 37

B
babies, 15, 18
blood tests, 6, 14, 15, 17
blood transfusions, 6, 17, 26, 32

C
Centers for Disease Control and Prevention (CDC), 13, 15, 28
children, 5, 6, 8, 9, 16, 22–25, 36
condoms, 19, 23, 35

D
drugs, 6, 17, 24, 25

E
epidemics, 11, 12–13, 21, 25
influenza (Spanish Influenza), 11
SARS (severe acute respiratory syndrome), 12–13

H
hemophilia, 26, 27, 31, 32
HIV (Human Immunodeficiency Virus), 6
possible origin of, 13–14
prevention, 17–18, 19
symptoms of, 15–17
transmission of, 6, 17–19
treatment of, 20

I
immune system, 6, 15, 38

J
Joint United Nations Programme on HIV/AIDS, 36

N
needles, 6, 17, 25

O
opportunistic illnesses, 6, 15
orphans, 6, 8–9, 24

P
pandemic, 11
poverty, 7, 22

R
Rescue/AIDS, 25

S
sexual activity, 6, 18–19, 22–23, 24, 30, 35

U
UNAIDS, 21, 25

V
vaccines, 36–37, 38

W
White, Ryan, 31–35, 38
World AIDS Day, 39–40

Z
zoonosis, 14